THERE ARE NO MONSTERS UNDER THE BED ?

Mesha BOLTON
Ayla VALIYEVA

This book belongs to

"Happily ever after,"
my Mommy said,
shutting the book
and tucking me in bed.

Now that my bedtime story has been read,
Mommy and Daddy
plant kisses on my head.

As they were about to leave,
I called out with dread,
"Before you turn off the light,
please check under the bed!"

"Whatever for?"
My Daddy asked,
as I pulled up my sheets,
covering my face like a mask.

"For monsters," I whispered,
and they both turned and laughed.
"We can take a look together,
if you're up for the task?"

So I jumped out of bed
and we began our hunt;

in search of sharp fangs,

angry ghosts,

and evil grunts.

But there were no monsters under the bed.

We checked around my room,
there were no three-eyed heads.

We peeked inside the hall closet,

even under the kitchen faucet,

but found no signs of the undead.

One last look in every nook.
I was beginning to be swayed.

Because all around the house,
it was quiet as a mouse.
Was there really no reason to be afraid?

"See? There are no such things as monsters,"
the monsters around us said,

all leaving the house
while shaking their heads.

I stared, open-mouthed,
up at my mom and dad.
"You heard what they said.
Now, go to bed!"

9 781778 210808